For Harry
M. W.

For Amy and Mike
P. D.

Text copyright © 2000 by Martin Waddell
Illustrations copyright © 2000 by Penny Dale

All rights reserved.

First U.S. edition 2000

Library of Congress Cataloging-in-Publication Data
Waddell, Martin.
Night, night Cuddly Bear / Martin Waddell ; illustrated by Penny Dale — 1st U.S. ed.
p.   cm.
Summary: Before he can go to bed, a young boy asks everyone in his family
if anyone has seen his teddy bear.
ISBN 0-7636-1195-6
[1. Bedtime—Fiction. 2. Teddy bears—Fiction. 3. Toys—Fiction.
4. Family life—Fiction.] I. Dale, Penny, ill. II. Title.

PZ7.W1137 Ni 2000
[E]—dc21 99-053125

2 4 6 8 10 9 7 5 3 1

Printed in Hong Kong

This book was typeset in OPTILucius AD.
The illustrations were done in colored pencil.

Candlewick Press
2067 Massachusetts Avenue
Cambridge, Massachusetts 02140

Night Night,
CUDDLY BEAR

Martin Waddell

illustrated by Penny Dale

CANDLEWICK PRESS
CAMBRIDGE, MASSACHUSETTS

It was bedtime
and Joe started playing his
Cuddly Bear game.
"Cuddly Bear's gone somewhere,"
Joe told Mommy. "We have to
ask everyone if they've seen him."
"Everyone?" Mommy said.
"Let's start with Daddy," said Joe.

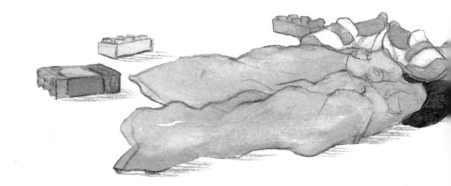

"Have you seen Cuddly Bear?"
Mommy asked Daddy.
"He vanished again,
    just before bedtime for Joe."

"Maybe he's gone on a boat
to Brazil," Daddy said.
"He knows lots of bears
there, and he's been
learning to row."

"I don't think so,"
said Joe.

"Have you seen
Cuddly Bear?"
Joe asked Paul.
"He might be at
the funfair,"
Paul said.
"Cuddly Bear
likes the swings
at the fair."

"I don't think so,"
said Joe.

"Have you seen Cuddly Bear?"
Mommy asked Sarah.
"We need him now because
Joe is going to bed."
"Maybe he went to Grandma's
house to climb trees,"
Sarah said. "Cuddly
Bear is a great
tree climber."

"I don't think
so," said Joe.

"No one has seen Cuddly Bear," Mommy said.
"We haven't asked everyone yet," said Joe.
Mommy asked Max the
Giraffe and Pojo and
Esmeralda but
they hadn't seen
Cuddly Bear.

"Night night, Esmeralda.
Night night, Pojo.
Night night, Max,"
said Joe.

"We've asked everyone now," Mommy said.
"You haven't asked me," said Joe.
"Have you seen Cuddly Bear,
  little Joe?" Mommy asked.

"He's upstairs taking his clothes off," Joe said.

"He's putting on his pajamas," Joe said.

"He's brushing his teeth in the bathroom," Joe said.

"He's in my room now, ready for bed," Joe said.

"I can't see Cuddly Bear!" Mommy said.
"He's hiding," said Joe. "He always
does this when I'm going to bed!"
"Hiding where?" Mommy said.
"You have to find him," said Joe.

"Is he in this room?" Mommy said.
"I think he must be,"
said Joe.

"Near your bed?" Mommy said.
"I think he might be,"
said Joe.

"Under your pillow?" said Mommy.
"I think he could be," said Joe.

"Got you, Cuddly Bear!" Mommy said.
"I knew Mommy would find you,"
Joe told Cuddly Bear. "She's the
best-ever bear finder there is."

Joe climbed into bed beside Cuddly Bear. Mommy told them a story, all about a small boy and his bear who rowed all the way to Brazil. They were captured by pirates but they escaped and got home before bedtime.

"Night night, Mommy,"
  said Joe.
"Night night, little Joe,"
  Mommy said.
"Night night, Cuddly Bear,"
  whispered Joe.

And Joe and his bear
went to sleep.